FORG(

The /ui

Murray Barber P. I.

Case

By

Julie Burns Sweeney

1

Copyright: 2017

Published by: Lulu.com

ISBN: 978-0-244-31166-7

CHAPTER ONE

Murray put down his coffee and stared at the middle-aged man sat opposite him. How was he supposed to deal with a case like this?

"I know you must think it's a risk Mr Barber, but I've got good clothes and just look at my watch... worth over four hundred pounds! In fact take it, take it as a down payment. I'm sure I'll be able to pay you, I must have money, I just need to find out who I am. Please help me Mr Barber."

Murray took the watch handed to him and placed it down on the table between them.

"You don't remember anything?" he asked.

"I woke up in hospital. I've read the police reports

about the accident but nothing rings any bells. I don't know who I had been with or even how we came by the car. Social services have tried to help me, they've put me in bed and breakfast and have sorted an allowance for me, all of which I will probably have to pay back but I can't live my life like this."

"The car you were found in had been reported stolen? What's happening about that Mr Smith."

"I couldn't give a statement as I can't remember. I've been told not to move away without notifying the police but I want to mention that my prints were not found in the car owner's home. Apparently the woman that owned the car had been in Spain, she came home to find she'd been burgled and her car taken. After I'd been taken to hospital the police ran a check on the car to find out who I was and found it was registered to this Maria Whiteshaw. She doesn't know me and nothing has come back to me in the last five months, I don't know where to go next."

"Ok." Murray let out a sigh and gave a reassuring smile to Mr Smith. "I'll give it a go but even if I find out who you are that doesn't necessarily mean you'll remember still. I'll need to see the police reports and I take it you didn't have any ID on you?"

"Wouldn't need you if I had. I've been given the full once over by the docs and there's nothing else wrong with me, I'm not on any regular medication or anything. I may be a criminal, a burglar? I really don't remember, but I doubt it, it just doesn't feel right."

"How do I know this watch isn't stolen Mr Smith?" Murray was starting to doubt the wisdom of his decision to take on this case. Mr Smith shrugged and sat back.

"It's all I've got at the moment. I don't know? The police took a look at it and they didn't seem worried about it."

"You say you've got a copy of the police reports?"

"Yes." Mr Smith pulled them out from a carrier bag on the seat beside him. "You're welcome to take them, I know them word for word but they just don't help me."

"Ok. What I'm going to do is this. I'll take the reports and I'll see how far I can get in a week. If I really can't find anything out, how your accident happened or get any closer to who you are by then, well then I may have to call it quits but I will try my very best. It's not something I've ever taken on before."

"I can't ask for more than that Mr Barber. Thankyou."

Once back at home, Murray sat himself down with the usual coffee and laid out the police report on his table.

"Right Mr Smith, let's see what we do know about you?" He glanced at the clock, one fifty, he had a husband up to no good to catch at five thirty. Mr Goodier was not returning home from work at the usual time anymore but this apparently was down to increased traffic. 'Yeah right!' as Mrs Beverleigh Goodier had said, 'he must think I'm such an idiot!'

An hour and a half from Kingsbridge to Plympton? It was a feeble excuse. So Murray was going to follow him home and check for any 'detours' as Mrs Goodier suspected. He reckoned if he left at four thirty he would have plenty of time to get to Kingsbridge, at most the trip should only take forty minutes.

So back to Mr Smith, found unconscious in the passenger seat of a Laguna off the road near Bolventor up on the moor. The car was found half turned over in a ditch at nine thirty in the evening. It could easily have been missed which meant no-one could say for sure how long it had been there. There was no sign of the driver, no blood trail, whether they were ok or not, the report couldn't say. Mr Len Williams had reported the accident after spotting the car on his way past. A concerned passer-by, no more. Murray made a note of the telephone number, a call wouldn't hurt, he had to start somewhere. Then there was the car itself. The registered owner was one Mrs Maria Whiteshaw from Okehampton. She apparently had been in Spain and only returned that day to find her house broken into and her car gone. She reported the car stolen at eight o'clock. Did that mean that Mr Smith and his accomplice had just stolen the vehicle and were heading west? Murray shook his head, surely that would mean the burglary was committed around tea time, not the best time with people returning home from work? He then stopped and re-read that part of the report again, the car was assumed to be going east. That made little sense,

Okehampton was well east of the moor. What or where were they going? Murray made a note of Mrs Whiteshaw's number and address and made a mental note to call upon the neighbours aswell to see whether they noticed what time the car had gone? The only statement from a neighbour was that of one Miss Hockey. She said she hadn't seen the car for days. Again Murray shook his head, maybe she just wasn't very observant? There wasn't a lot to go on. Murray sat back and picked up the watch that Mr Smith had given him. No inscription but it did feel heavy. Expensive? Maybe he could take it in to a jeweller's and get an opinion on where it might have come from? There wasn't anything in the report about it. Finally, Murray made a note of the officer involved, maybe his mate Jeff from

C.I.D. could track him down and let Murray have a chat with him too?

He decided there was no time like the present to get started, he was taking Indian over to Jenny's after he had followed Mr Goodier home so he didn't want to be working late. He picked up the phone and dialled the number he had jotted down for Mr Williams.... He wasn't home according to his wife. 'Never got in before seven'. Murray gave her his mobile number and asked if her husband could get back to him? So much for taking the evening off!

He didn't want to give up so easily, so next on the list was Maria Whiteshaw. The conversation started off friendly enough until Murray explained who had hired him and why he had called, Maria then became quite coy.

"...I'm sorry Mr Barber, I really don't think there is anything else I can add to what I told the police. And we still haven't got our stuff back."

"I take it there'd be no chance of bringing Mr Smith around to your house to see if it jogs his memory?" Murray was pulling a face, even he wouldn't have said yes.

"I don't want that man in my house. Everything was said in the report. We came home from Spain on the ten o'clock flight, and when we got home my car had gone and the back window had been broken and our stuff had gone. The car was scrapped, not that I would have wanted it back anyway."

"What time did you get in? I mean, was there any sign of when the robbery took place?"

"Err... We hadn't come straight home... we went

shopping first, got some food in. It must have been about seven... quarter to eight when we got in." Did she sound a little flustered? Murray wondered if they had upped the insurance claim? Although if the driver had the car key then there must have been a robbery. He didn't want to waste her time anymore, he had the report and he could always get back to her if he needed to, as long as she would talk to him that was? He thanked her for her co-operation and ended the call.

He sat back and stared once more at the police reports. Was there something he was missing? So far he couldn't get past the car and where it might have been going... or coming from? He wanted to speak to Miss Hockey and get a look at the layout of the street. If Mr Smith had been a known criminal then his prints would have been on file. They

weren't. So.... either this was a first time crime or

Mr Smith had never been caught.. for anything. A

thought crossed Murray's mind, maybe the amnesia

was an act to get someone to help 'Mr Smith' find

his evasive partner? He shook his head and grabbed

his keys and camera, that didn't sit right. Mr Smith,

good or bad, could wait for now as Mr Goodier

would soon be finishing work...

CHAPTER TWO

Mr Goodier left his place of work promptly at five-thirty and headed straight towards the main road back to Plymton. Murray had already fixed his phone into his hands-free cradle on his dashboard just in case Mr Williams, the roadside rescuer, called. The phone did ring, just as Mr Goodier turned down a side road on the edge of Kingsbridge but it wasn't Mr Williams, it was Jenny.

"Hi hun, just checking you're ok?" Her voice was bright, a little like her copper-coloured hair which had been dyed that colour to match a particular outfit.

"Yeah, still on for later?"

"Is that ok? Or are you working, you had a meeting with some guy didn't you?"

"Yeah. Lost his memory, wants to know who he is. I'll tell you about it later. What do you want from the Spice Palace?" Murray was still following Mr Goodier who now pulled into the driveway of a semi-detached house.

"How can he pay if he doesn't know who he is?.. Oh, never mind I'm sure you'll explain! Erm..I'll have my usual please! What are you doing now?"

"Just watching a man undo his marriage."

"Oh dear, another one of those cases? ... You're not driving are you? I don't want to cause an accident..."

"No, no! I've pulled in now but you're on the hands-free don't panic!" Murray had lifted his camera and was discreetly filming the woman at the house who was now welcoming Mr Goodier into her home. Murray took note of the address so he could find out her identity later once he was back home.

Some thirty-five minutes later Murray filmed Mr Goodier reappearing from the semi and once more heading in the direction of home. He didn't stop again and after a visit to the Spice Palace, Murray reached Jenny's house-share by seven forty-five. Just as the Merlot was poured and the plates placed on the kitchen table, Mr Williams finally rang.

"... I'm sorry to bother you with this Mr Williams, it's just that the man who was in that crashed car still hasn't regained his memory and he's asked for my help..."

"Oh, I see. I'm afraid there's not much I can tell you. I was driving home and thought I caught sight of the rear of the car in my headlights, they were dipped as another car had just gone passed. To be honest, I had driven on about half a mile before I decided to turn around and go back and check what I'd seen. You know what it's like, you don't expect to see a car off the road. Anyway, there he was, not even strapped into his seat... he was in the passenger seat, did you know that?"

"Yes, yes I did. There wasn't any sign of the driver then?"

"No... no didn't see anyone else, just him, out cold. I stayed until they took him away in the ambulance and gave the police a statement the next day."

"One last thing, which way do you think the car had been going, east or west?"

"Oh, east, definitely. There were skid marks along the road. When I came back you could see them clear as day in my beams. Weaving along the road they were like the car was out of control...."

"Well that was interesting." Murray sat back down with Jenny and prepared to tuck into his lamb Rogan Josh. "According to him, the car was out of control before it went off the road."

"Der! They would hardly have driven off the road on purpose!" Jenny stated the obvious.

"Well yes! But why was it out of control?" He raised his eyebrows at her sarcastic grin. "Was it a fault with the car or was there an argument going on inside the car?"

"Trouble amongst thieves, eh?"

"Mmm." He finished his mouthful. "And where were they going?.... Maybe they had just finished another job? I suppose they thought they were safe for a while with the car if they knew the owners were away and wouldn't have reported it stolen yet?"

"What did the car's owner have to say?"

"Not a lot! Says they came back on the morning flight and found the car gone and the house broken into."

"Where is the car now?"

"Err... dunno? Have to check the report when I get home. Think she said it had been scrapped.... She was a bit queer about her day... said they came back on the ten o'clock flight but didn't get home till nearly eight that night. Something about food shopping on the way back?"

"Clothes shopping, shoe shopping, even house shopping but food shopping? For how long?"

"I know, it sounded odd at the time? But why

should she have lied about what time they got back?... The only reason I could think of was maybe they were upping the insurance claim?"

"You mean, maybe they didn't lock up as well as they should and 'fixed' the situation before calling the police?"

"Something like that. But it doesn't change the situation for Mr Smith." Murray took a long sip of his wine just as his mobile rang again. "Murray Barber, private investigator.... Oh, hello Aunt Pam! How are you?" He winked at Jenny as she waved as though to say 'hello'. "We'd love to come to dinner Aunty but Jenny's off for a couple of days tomorrow... yes her 'high flying' job! ... London... Yes, I'm fine now I just wish everyone would stop asking.... the new car's great.. yes... I will, yes. Ok....

I'll see you tomorrow evening then... take care Aunty..." He hung up and smiled at Jenny. "She sends her love! Looks like I'm eating at hers tomorrow night!"

"Don't go looking for any buried bodies then!"

"Ha ha! Where were we?"

"Skid marks. Surely..." Jenny waved her fork above her plate. ".. those skid marks would have been seen in daylight?"

"Probably? But to be honest, I wouldn't stop for skid marks... What? You don't think it had been there long?" Jenny shook her head and shrugged.

"I don't know? Was the engine warm?"

"Good point. No idea! I'm gonna re-read that report when I get home and give Jeff a call, see if I can have a word with the officer's involved."

"You in a rush to get home?" She was pouring the wine again.....

CHAPTER THREE

Murray arrived home early the next morning to find his answer phone flashing at him. There was a message from a Mr Mason of Mason Couriers, 'could Mr Barber please return his call?' Murray jotted down the contact number and glanced at the clock. He'd have a coffee first and phone back after eight thirty. He then picked up the police report that Mr Smith had given him. It was six pages long, a copy of the details that the police thought were relevant for Mr Smith to know. He flicked through until he found the section on the car. 'Assumed travelling east', mmm, he knew why that was now, skid marks on the road. Ah, here it was, the engine was cold! Cold? So it must have been there a while? Which meant the accident must have happened at least before ... eight? No, he shook his head, he was trying to link two different things together, the accident happened whenever it happened and Mrs Whiteshaw reported the burglary once she'd got home... and possibly arranged the evidence? The two things weren't connected.... So what was it that was bothering him?

So what about the missing driver? The report said that the steering wheel had been wiped so no fingerprints. Typical! Same with the door handles, but plenty of prints in the car generally. Mrs Whiteshaw's and many others, apparently she was given to taking friends out and about on a regular basis, so probably family and friends. Tucked in the back of the file was a copy of a photograph. Murray hadn't taken much notice of it at first glance but now he studied it closely. It was of the car in its position in the ditch. Taken from the driver side with the door open, something struck Murray, the seat was well forward. A short man? Or maybe ... a woman?

He gulped down the last mouthful of coffee and dialled Mason's number. Mr Mason was a very plain speaking man who was not happy that deliveries from his south west depot were not arriving intact. Parcels were arriving sealed but with items missing. Originally this had gone back to where ever they had been dispatched from but as the trend had continued and happened to more than one company, things had to be looked into. Mr Mason, or at least his manager, had whittled the choice of culprit down to two men, however without evidence of their thefts, they couldn't deal with the matter as they wished. When they put other men on with the two drivers, nothing went missing but business didn't allow for double staffing. Could Murray follow the men, one each day, until they were spotted opening and resealing parcels and gather some concrete evidence for a prosecution? Of course he could, that's what he did, it was his thing! He took all the relevant details and arranged to be outside the depot at eight the next morning to follow the first of the two drivers.

Next, Murray started a quick address search for the identity of Mr Goodier's extra-marital call on his way home from work the previous night. While the computer searched, he dialled Jeff's number.

"Alright Murray?"

"I am! Are you?" Murray jotted down the lady's name that popped up on his screen.

"Good, good. What's up?"

"Do you know anything about this amnesia case from five months ago? A Mr Smith found unconscious in a stolen car out near Bolventor?"

"Vaguely? Not one of mine though. You onto it are you?" Jeff was laughing, not for the first time was he amused by the jobs Murray landed himself with.

"Yeah. Strange one for sure. I was just wondering whether you could get me a meeting with the officers involved? I've got the reports but it's never the same."

"Can you give us their names?"

"Erm..." Murray dragged the report over his keyboard and read out the names. "Barker and.... Martin. Oh, and one other thing, do you know where the car was scrapped? I wouldn't mind taking Mr Smith along to have another look at it, see if it jogs any memories."

"I'll look into it. Anything else?"

"How's Kate?"

"Doing well!" Jeff's wife, Kate, was reaching the six month marker of her pregnancy.

After one last call to Mrs Goodier about her husband and sending her an e-mail with the footage he had taken the evening before, Murray decided it was time to go and visit the scene of the burglary or at least the neighbours. He couldn't help but feel Maria Whiteshaw was a little nervous of him, so he thought he best not push it too much, but a look at how tall she was wouldn't be a bad thing.

He climbed in his car and started his engine.

"Murray my man! What's going on, anything exciting?" Murray glanced in his rearview mirror.

"Ali! Where have you been hiding?"

"Just 'cos you can't see us doesn't mean we're hiding!" Ali was laughing in the back seat.

"Hello Rita, you must be here too then?" Murray still stared in his empty mirror.

"Hello Murray! Where are we off to?"

"Uh, where to start? I've got a man with no memory who was found in a stolen crashed car who wants to know who he is...."

"Not the usual then?" Rita sounded amused.

"No." Murray had driven out of the resident's carpark and was heading in the direction of Okehampton and Maria Whiteshaw's street. "Don't suppose you two have a magic answer to amnesia?"

"Sorry mate. Anything else on?"

"Erm... yeah... light-fingered courier. ...Actually..." As Murray concentrated on his driving he considered whether or not it would be helpful taking these two along with him on the Mason case? "I might beable to use you two tomorrow, if you're up for a bit of surveillance that is?"

"Following a delivery van?" Rita had sat forward and was now right behind Murray's left ear.

"Well, if he's raiding his parcels, he's not gonna do it in broad daylight, he'll probably hide in the back of the van. Could do with some x-ray eyes."

"Ok Murray mate, we'll be there. What time you leaving?"

"Be out the house by seven thirty. Is that ok?"

"We don't keep office hours Murray darling!" Murray smiled in his mirror towards his left shoulder where Rita's voice was coming from.

By the time they pulled into the end of Maria's road, which turned out to be a cul-de-sac, they had made a plan of action. Ali and Rita were going to see if Maria was home and estimate her height, checking her new car if necessary, and Murray was going in search of Miss Hockey. He glanced at the detached house across the road as he casually strolled up the path to number six. Stood on the drive infront of the garage was a new Honda, brand new according to the registration. The front garden was neat, if somewhat suburban, and the windows all had matching nets hanging at them.

"And a villa in Spain!" Murray muttered to himself as he turned and took in Miss Hockey's home. It too was neatly kept but the blinds and curtains didn't match and the car was five... no seven years old. He rang the bell...

A lad in his late teens answered the door with earphones hanging around his neck.

"Yeah?" he asked sounding barely interested in an

answer.

"Is Miss Hockey home please?"

"Nah, she's gone to work. Who wants her?"

"Er.. I'm a private investigator, here's my card..." Murray pulled one of his cards out from the back of his wallet and handed it over to the young man. "I was just wondering if I could ask Miss Hockey some questions about the burglary that took place over at Mrs Whiteshaw's house some months ago? I've been hired by the man who was found in the car..."

"Oh yeah! I remember all that. They asked me Mum if she'd seen anything." The lad was reading Murray's card. "Can she give you a call then?"

"That'd be great if she would. Do you recall anything?"

"The car wasn't there." He stated it as a matter of

fact as he stared across the road at Maria's house. "They'd gone to their place in Spain and left the car on the drive, like her car is now, but it had long gone before they came home, days like!"

"It wasn't stolen the day they reported it then?" The two of them were studying each other.

"Nah, it had definitely gone at least a couple of days before. Not many people come up this turning..." Murray could almost see the lad's cogs turning inside his mind. "... Don't think anyone remembers seeing anyone strange hanging about watching the place. It was odd, them being done over, know what I mean?"

"Well, you mean no-one else has had any trouble like that?"

"Not since we lived here." The lad took a step

backwards. "I'll give me Mum this, ok."

"Thanks. That'd be great." Murray turned and walked slowly back to his car. Miss Hockey's lad seemed brighter than he sounded, why should someone pick on that particular house out of the blue? Something was a little off about that burglary. Did Maria Whiteshaw know Mr Smith? Maybe, if it had all been an insurance scam? Was that why she didn't want to see him? Incase he remembered her and what she'd asked him to do? But surely if that was the case he wouldn't say anything, it wouldn't be to his advantage? Murray shook his head and climbed back into his car to wait for Ali and Rita. He didn't wait more than ten minutes.

"You were quick!" Rita's voice was bouncing around the back of Murray's car.

"Yeah man! Thought you'd be ages?"

"Miss Hockey's not home. Spoke to her son and he says the same as she did in her statement, the car was gone days before."

"Really?" Ali was sat beside Murray in the front as the engine was started and the car moved away in the direction of home once more.

"Mmm... What about Maria Whiteshaw? Was she home?"

"Yes, she was there, chatting away on the phone. To her sister I think but I wasn't really listening."

"I thought all women liked a bit of gossip on the phone?" Murray teased.

"Shut up Murray! Actually she was telling her sister to go to Spain, go and stay at the villa."

"Was she tall or short?" Murray was still thinking

about the seat position in the crashed car.

"Quite tall."

"About five eight, five nine I'd reckon Murray mate."

"Mmm, probably not our driver then?"

"Do you really think she had been driving? She was in Spain at the time, wasn't she?"

Murray glanced in his rearview mirror.

"I don't know what I'm thinking. The police report says she was on the morning flight home that day, so yes, she should have been in Spain. Although it looks now like the car was taken a few days before. I don't know if that matters or not?" Murray felt as though his brain was tying itself into a knot.

"The car couldn't have been crashed in that ditch for a few days Man. Someone would have reported it long before it was reported."

"That's true. Which means Maria Whiteshaw wasn't the driver when it crashed. So what have we got? The house is burgled and the car taken and then a few days later the Whiteshaws return and report the burglary and on the same day the car crashes and Mr Smith has no memory."

"It is all a bit odd. I mean, it could just be coincidence but it does sound odd."

"Yeah, I agree Rita, something just doesn't seem quite right.... but what?"

CHAPTER FOUR

Having washed and changed, Murray pulled up in his Aunt Pam's parking spot outside her old harbourside cottage ready to tuck into one of her delicious home-made meals. The sea wind hit him hard as he climbed out of the car and approached the front door. His Aunt threw her arms around him and welcomed him inside in her usual enthusiastic manner. He in return embraced both her and the warmth of her thick-walled home, and the aroma of chicken and sage drifting out from the kitchen.

"Pity Jenny couldn't make it, you two make such a lovely couple. Come through, get yourself warmed up by the rayburn." Murray followed her through to the kitchen to find she wasn't alone. "Oh, this is my friend Jo-anna, she's joining us for tea. Jo dear, this is my nephew Murray."

"Oh the private investigator. Hello."

"Hello, nice to meet you." Suddenly he felt he was being set up, not for the first time by his dear Aunt.

"Now, we want to ask you Murray, are you very busy at the moment?" Pam was pouring out coffee into three mugs.

"Reasonably, why? What's up Aunty?" Murray sat himself down at the kitchen table opposite Jo-anna and waited.

"Well, Jo-anna here lives up at Tremeara...."

"It's a rest home, for us olden's!" Jo-anna smiled.

"Things are going missing Murray, I know, it sounds like something out of comic book! Old dears losing things! But however silly it sounds, it's becoming very upsetting for some of the residents."

"I should think it's very frustrating." Murray smiled sympathetically. "But surely the managers are dealing with it?"

"Karen just thinks we're being forgetful. Oh, she's being very nice about it but she's not taking us seriously." Jo was animated. "Thing is, there's no-one new around. No new staff and no new residents. So where's our stuff going?"

It was a good question. Murray studied Jo-anna. She didn't look gaga.

"What's gone missing? I take it there's more than one person's stuff involved?"

"Oh yes. I think the first person to mention anything was Darcy, she couldn't find her gold

41

cross. She always placed it in her jewellery box on her dresser every night, but then it just disappeared. We searched and Tina and Gill helped, they're the morning staff, but we never did find it. Then I think it was Tom who lost his father's pocket watch. He had got it out for its monthly silver polish, he's very particular, and it had gone from his wooden box that he keeps in the bottom of his wardrobe. He did make a fuss but again, with everyone having a good search, it was never found. Then just last week Barbara lost her cameo ring right off her finger! She's actually bedridden and on her way to loco-land but once again, even with the staff completely stripping her bed down and searching her clothing, it hasn't been found."

"People may get forgetful in their later years

Murray, but it's more than a coincidence what's going on over there. Do you think you could find time to have a nose around?" Pam had joined them at the table and was looking expectantly at Murray.

"Well...." he sat back. "You can't all be losing your marbles, or your jewellery! It does sound a little odd doesn't it?... Ok, I'll come over and have a chat with your friends, that is, if your manager doesn't mind?"

"Karen? No, she won't mind. She'll probably tell you you're wasting your time though, she thinks it will all turn up soon enough, when we remember where we really left everything!"

"It's quite patronizing. She should be taking it seriously." Pam got up again and opened the oven and lifted out a crispy, delicious looking cooked chicken. Murray tried not to get distracted as the food was about to be plated up.

"I've got a job on tomorrow but I could pop over in the evening, not too late?"

"They try to have us in bed by nine but we rarely are!" Jo-anna let out a gentle but rebellious giggle.

"You say there's no new staff or residents?"

"No. No-one new."

"Mmm? That would have been the obvious choice. I take it the 'thief' must be mobile, so that'll rule out all those that need assistance. What about the staff? Anyone a bit untrustworthy?"

"No. That's just the problem you see. We can't work out what's going on. We're a happy bunch. The staff are helpful and friendly and we all get along. But who knows how long that will last if things keep going missing?"

"Well, don't worry. I'll come over tomorrow and you can introduce me to everyone. See if I can spot who's acting guilty!"

Over dinner Jo-anna went on to tell Murray about Tremeara and its general set up. The building was a former hotel which had been adapted to house the elderly, of which there were presently fourteen. Apart from Karen there were four full-time staff and two ancillary staff. Meals were delivered from a local meal service. The resident's all had their own rooms and en-suites, basic but at least they were private. A number of the residents were suffering with immobility of one sort or another. The only one's which were probably agile enough to get around and sneak in and out of rooms were Byron,

Tom, Cathy, Darcy, Lizzie, Cyril and Jo-anna. Murray tried to keep a mental track of what he was being told but decided he had just better go armed with notebook and pen the following evening.

Having had his fill of his Aunt's home-cooking, Murray offered to run Jo-anna back to Tremeara which would enable him to get a quick look at the place. As he drove into the front driveway Murray found that although it had once been a hotel, Tremeara was not nearly as large or as grand as he had imagined. It stood detached within its own plot of land, the gardens around it looking neat and cared for and the view down over the town and out to sea quite spectacular. Overall the place let off a homely feel.

CHAPTER FIVE

Murray was up and about early the next morning
which, considering he had once again sat outside
Michelle's terraced home desperately trying to
decide whether or not to knock for well over an
hour before finally watching the lights inside go out
and driving home alone, was somewhat surprising
but he had work to do and a courier van to follow.
He gathered his camera and a couple of chocolate
bars from the fridge and headed out into the bitter
morning air. Hopefully Ali and Rita wouldn't be far
away and the case would be solved nice and quickly,
Murray was only too aware that he'd only given
himself a week to make some sort of promising

progress with Mr Smith. If he could keep his mind on the cases in hand then maybe the urge, and the guilt that went with it, to start seeing Michelle again would die away?

Climbing into his car he was met with a greeting from some things that had already died, Ali and Rita.

"Murray mate, you're late!"

"Am not! Morning Rita or are you alone Ali?" Murray glanced quickly in his mirror as he started the engine and threw on the heater to warm the car.

"Hello Murray, how's your Aunt?"

"As demanding as ever! She's got another job for me, no bodies involved this time though, just missing possessions!"

"What about your man with the missing identity

Murray mate?" Murray glanced again in his rearview mirror as he filed into the stream of early morning commuter traffic.

"To be honest, I don't really know how I'm supposed to find out who he is. Something funny's going on with the whole business but I can't quite put my finger on it. It'd really help if he could remember something... anything."

"Isn't that the whole point?" Murray could just picture Rita's eyebrows rising in the seat behind him. "What are you going to do about him?"

"Well..." Murray watched the road as he spoke. "... I need to find the car and get him back inside it if possible, try and trigger something familiar. It's the only place we have that we know he's been before.... Other than the burgled house... but apart from the fact we're not likely to get him back in there, I'm not convinced that that house or the burglary are all that important.... It would be handy to know who the driver was mind."

Murray pulled in to the kerb opposite the depot and waited for the vans to leave. He flicked through his notebook until he found his notes with the relevant number plate written down. Glancing back across the road he spotted the said van so sat back and waited. The ring of his mobile broke through the sound of the passing traffic.

"Murray Barber, private investigator."

"Hello, Mr Barber, I'm sorry to bother you so early but I just got your message from my son. They're useless at passing on anything that's not in text form!"

"Ah... Miss Hockey?" Murray quickly put a name to the lady's voice at the other end of the line. "No problem, I'm up and out! Thanks for calling. Did your son explain that I've been asked to try and identify the man who was found in your neighbour's stolen car?"

"He muttered something this morning as he left! Something about when the car went?"

"Yeah, do you by any chance remember the car being there? It's a while ago now."

"Err... it's a bit blurry but I do remember what I said at the time. The car had definitely gone before the day Maria and Jim returned from their Spanish villa, she makes a big deal about going over to Spain, like we all care! I'd say it had gone a good three or four days before. Never realized the house had been broken into though, not the sort of thing that ever happens around here."

"Mmm, strange then?"

"Odd definitely. Makes you wonder if it was someone who knew them? Not one of the neighbours, but someone who knew they were away."

"Any ideas by any chance?"

"No, sorry."

"Did you ever see the man found in the crashed car, Mr Smith as he goes by now?" Murray watched as a man approached the van in the depot opposite.

"No, no never saw him, or a picture or anything. Is he ok then?"

"Amnesia, still! Maybe at some point I'll bring a photo over if that's ok? It's just a long shot?"

"No problem but mornings are better."

As the man over the road climbed into the van and started the engine, Murray politely ended his call with Miss Hockey and started his own engine ready to follow the van on its deliveries.

"So what did she say Murray?" He glanced in his mirror briefly before answering Rita.

"Just that the car had gone days before the Whiteshaws returned and reported it."

"Does that mean anything?"

"Not really." Murray shrugged and pulled in again as the driver had reached his first drop-off already. "I wish I knew who the driver was who was with Mr Smith. I thought for some unfathomable reason that perhaps Mrs Whiteshaw was involved, just because of the position of the seat, but she can't be, not the driver anyhow. But even Miss Hockey just said maybe the Whiteshaws knew the burglars... or at least the burglars knew they were away. The question is... does Mr Smith know the Whiteshaws?... Or do they know him? ... Or does the driver know them or do they know who the driver was?"

"Lot of questions man."

"And no answers Ali!"

The van took off again and Murray once again followed. It made two more stops before Murray's phone rang once more. He slipped it into the handsfree holder fixed to his dashboard and answered it. It was Jeff calling from his desk at the police station.

"Murray, I've found your car. The crashed one? It

was taken out to Campions Scrap Yard. Just east of town, you know it?"

"Oh yeah. Do you know if it was crushed or just scrapped?"

"No idea, sorry. Give 'em a call."

"Will do, thanks again!"

"No luck yet then?"

"Nothing of any use. Can I speak to the officer who dealt with the case yet?"

"I gave him your number... er, Barker. He said he'll give you a call, he wrote up the notes."

"Great, I'll catch up with you later." Once more the van was on the move.

"This is gonna be a long day Murray man."

"He'll have to stop soon or else there'll be nothing left in his van to raid!" And just as Murray spoke the van turned right at the traffic lights and parked up in the supermarket carpark. They sat and waited while the driver went and bought himself some lunch and a paper and then returned to his van. He didn't climb back into his cab however, but instead opened his rear doors which were facing the planted shrubbery at the edge of the carpark. From what Murray could see, he then sat on the back step and started on his lunch while moving some of the parcels around within the back of the van.

"Ok folks. Looks like we could be in business!" With his camera in his pocket, he got out of the car and stretched. "I'm gonna go for a walk up the pavement outside the carpark there and see if I can get a look down through the bushes. Keep an eye on him for us."

"Sure mate."

From beyond the bushes Murray could see the driver picking carefully at the wrapping on one of the boxes within his van. He wasn't even paying much attention to what was going on around him. Glancing around him, Murray noted there was some passing traffic but he was able to simply take out his camera and catch on film the driver removing what looked like some computer games from within the parcel and then reseal it. It was that simple! He returned to the car and checked what he had filmed to make sure he had caught all that he needed to. He then called Mr Mason who asked what drops had been made and asked Murray to bring the film back to the office.

Once the film was dropped, Murray returned

home and called the scrap yard. Yes the car was still there and no it hadn't been crushed but the engine had been removed along with various other parts. That wasn't going to be a problem so Murray then called Mr Smith and arranged to pick him up on the way out to the yard. Maybe he wouldn't remember anything but it was worth a try. He had just under two hours before he had to pick up Smith which mean't it was now or never. He picked up his keys and headed out the door.

Within ten minutes he was stood on Michelle's front doorstep and before he could give himself a chance to change his mind, he had rang the bell. To his surprise however, it wasn't Michelle who answered, it was a short shaven-haired man who stared at Murray questioningly.

"Is Michelle in?" Murray managed to ask.

"Yeah, 'Chelle. Someone here for you." She appeared quickly from behind the man's shoulder and stepped outside pulling the door close to behind her.

"Sorry." Murray's hands were shoved deep into his trouser pockets, he was feeling awkward, the last thing he had expected was for someone else to be on the scene. "I didn't mean to call at the wrong time, I should've called first..."

"Don't worry, you weren't to know. It is a bad time though. Can I call you later?"

"Yeah, sure. Jenny's not back till tomorrow..."

"Ok. I'll speak to you later." She cut him short and turned back towards her front door. With a shrug, Murray wandered back across the road to his car.

How could he have been so stupid? Why should he have assumed that she wouldn't have started seeing anyone else? He felt like an idiot. He started the car and drove off in the direction of Mr Smith's bed and breakfast, he might just aswell arrive early instead of returning home.

Murray sat outside Mr Smith's lodgings in his car for half an hour, slowly driving himself mad thinking about Michelle. He wasn't sure if he was jealous, angry or just feeling plain stupid. In the end he decided to give Smith a call and see if he was ready to go.

Twenty minutes later and the two men were on their way to Campion's Scrapyard. Smith was either nervous or excited, or maybe a little of both? Murray watched him fidgeting in his seat and wondered what it must be like to have no memory of who you are or what your life is really like. Somehow, with the recent meeting on Michelle's doorstep still all too fresh in his mind, Murray actually felt quite jealous.

"Do you remember what you were wearing when they found you in the car?" Murray asked.

"Er.. yeah. Cotton shirt and jeans. Slip-on designer pumps but no socks."

"No jacket?"

"No. At least they didn't find one. Probably would have had my wallet in it."

"Mmm? Do you think whoever was driving took it then or maybe you didn't have one with you?"

"It was the middle of winter! Bloody freezing apparently! If I didn't have one with me I have no idea why!"

"You say you haven't been back near the car since?"

"Nope. Had no idea what happened to it and it wasn't mine anyhow."

"Do you remember the car at all?" Murray turned into the entrance of the yard and switched off his engine.

"No. Something posh."

"Right. Well let's go and find out where it is and hope it jogs something." They got out of the car and with the help of the man in the office, they found the dented and really quite badly damaged Laguna. It was parked on the ground rather than on top of another vehicle like some of the others which was to their advantage as it meant that they could climb inside without the risk of hurting themselves.

"Get in then. You were found in the passenger seat so you take that side." Murray opened the driver door to find the seat still well forward. Should he try and fit in it? He might aswell, anything to help get a reaction from Mr Smith. Once they were both sat inside, Murray having to reluctantly adjust his seat, he turned to Mr Smith and asked if anything at all struck him? Smith stared at the dashboard, out through the windscreen and sat back and closed his eyes and took a deep breath.

"It's just so frustrating! I feel angry!" He paused and glared around the inside of the car again. "I feel like I know this car.... I can't put my finger on it..... but there's something familiar? No, I don't know..." The frustration was sounding in his voice but

Murray was hopeful. It wasn't much but it was enough, it had nudged a slight reaction.

"Anything on who your companion might have been?" There was another pause as Smith stared down at the driver's seat which Murray was still sat upon.

"No..." He said it very slowly and watching the man's expression, Murray wondered if he had recalled something?

"Are you sure?" Murray asked.

"Huh...!" He let out a long sigh. "A woman? I don't know if I'm just filling in the gaps with my imagination? My first thought was a woman, a blonde woman... But am I just pulling that from a scene in a film or something?"

"I think your first instinct is the best thing we can

go with. The more you think about it afterwards the more you'll doubt yourself. But that doesn't mean your first thought was fake." Murray took a deep breath. "So, so far we have the possibility of you and a blonde woman with some friction in this 'familiar' car. I think we've come a long way."

"Really?" A bemused sounding Mr Smith sat back and stared out of the windscreen. "I suppose it's something but it doesn't add up to much does it?"

"Well... ok. Let's retrace your steps, you're not in a hurry to get back are you?"

"Whatever for?"

"Right. It's not dark yet so, we don't know where you were after the car was taken until the crash but we do know where the car came from. Now, Mrs Whiteshaw doesn't want to meet you but that doesn't mean we can't drive in and out of the cul-de-sac. Come on, let's go!"

They climbed out of the wreck and walked back to Murray's car, thanking the man in the office as they passed. By the time they reached Okehampton the daylight was starting to disappear. Murray wasn't one hundred per cent sure of the way, was it the first or second turn after the large pub on the main road? He let out groaning sounds as he stared at the street names and got tooted from behind as he slowed.

"The second turn and then follow the road around to the left and take the steep right up the hill...." Mr Smith stopped abruptly with his arm still limply held in mid-air infront of him. "How do I know that? How the bloody hell do I know where we're going?"

"Bugger me?" Murray could barely concentrate on his driving. Who'd have thought such a simple thing could trigger such a reaction? "You must have driven this route a good many times for it to be so deeply ingrained. You either know the Whiteshaws or someone who lives very near them, like in the same street?" Mr Smith was sitting with a frown etched onto his face but the harder he tried to recall anything the more blurred his memory became. "Don't force it Mr Smith but it anything, anything at all strikes you, just say so."

Murray turned into the cul-de-sac and drove slowly passed the Whiteshaw's house towards the end. He deliberately didn't point out their house just to see if Smith himself could recognize it.

"Well?" he finally asked his silently frowning

passenger.

"That house over there... Is that the house?" He

was infact pointing at the right house.

"What about that house?"

"Paella? I can taste paella? They were in Spain

weren't they? That's their house isn't it?"

"Yep. That is their house. Are you sure you don't

know them?"

"Maybe? It sounds like it doesn't it?"

"You know, it did cross my mind that it was Maria

that was in the car with you. I know it doesn't make

much sense, they were in Spain, but do you recall

anything about the driver yet?"

"I don't know.... Sorry, this must be as frustrating

for you as it is for me."

"Don't worry about it. I've got one more idea."
Murray drove out of the cul-de-sac and headed back
towards the main road. He went west as the fog
drifted over the dark moor, his beams barely able to
follow the edge of the road. The famous Jamaica
Inn loomed out of the fog and then faded back into
it again. As they neared the area of the accident he
glanced sideways at Smith. Would he see a reaction
here? Not being completely sure where the accident
took place, Murray didn't stop but continued on
until finally they reached Bodmin. Only then did
Smith sit up and start studying his surroundings.

"What? You recognize something?"

"Erm...? I know this place.... Wadebridge! I know
Wadebridge!"

"What do you mean?"

"I... I think I live in Wadebridge."

Murray took the turning and followed the signs to Wadebridge. The fog had lifted here and the roads were much easier to see. They drove along the edge of the river, across the bridge and around some of the streets. Smith sat in the passenger seat pointing out different shops and restaurants, he seemed to know the town very well.

"So which way is home?" Murray asked as casually as he could, almost sliding the question anonymously into the conversation.

"Go back across the bridge and head left." Smith sounded thoughtful. Murray followed his instructions and let him lead by instinct. They soon found themselves outside a large house on the edge of the town. Murray pulled in by the gate and turned to Mr Smith.

"Well, we might just as well try knocking while we're here." They both got out of the car and strolled apprehensively up the path to the front door. Neither the bell nor loud knocks brought anyone to answer the door. No-one was home.

"Do you think I'm not home maybe?" Smith smiled.

"It's a nice house. You did say you had nice clothes?" Murray turned and walked back to his car. "Come on. I'll take you back to the B & B and you can sleep on this. You just might beable to fit some of these pieces together. I'll look up who lives here and hopefully the name will mean something to you."

"We're leaving?"

"We can't do anything now. What...? You think we're gonna break in? I do my detecting legally I'm afraid!"

By the time Murray finally got home it was gone nine. He had text message from Jenny on his mobile saying 'goodnight and sorry she hadn't called but the city air had given her a headache and she was going straight to bed'. He sent a quick message back and, kicking off his shoes, flopped onto his settee with his laptop and started a search for the address in Wadebridge. As he did so his mobile rang, glancing at the caller ID, he saw it was Michelle.

"Hi."

"Hi Murray, sorry about earlier." She sounded

tired but he could also hear the sound of someone else in the background.

"Look, you don't have to apologize. I should have phoned first..."

"No, no you didn't. I'm sorry about him, that was my ex-husband.... James can you put the rubbish out back and make sure the back kitchen door is locked, thanks. Sorry Murray, we're just finishing up for the night."

"You at work still?"

"Yeah. You working or are you at home?"

"Just got in. What did your ex want... or is that none of my business?" Murray wasn't sure if he should feel relieved or not.

"Uh..him. He thought he should tell me face to face that he's just got engaged to his floosy, just incase I hear it through the grapevine! You timed it pretty well actually, it left him wondering what I was up to! Bastard! I don't miss him!"

"I'm sorry if he's trying to give you a hard time."

"Ah, I'm not worried by him. I'm well and truly over him!.... So, how's things with you? Why did you come over anyhow?"

"I did ask if I could explain myself, what with the accident and all. I left you up in the air, it wasn't fair of me."

"Well... do you want to come over tonight? I'm heading home in about ten minutes."

"You ok with that?" The search had completed on his computer but Murray wasn't paying any attention to it.

"Sure, why not? I could do with the company..."

Making a quick note of the names that had

appeared on his screen, Murray shut down his

laptop, picked up his keys and headed back out of

the door.

CHAPTER SIX

Murray sat with his coffee in his hands staring out

through the ceiling to floor glass that stretched

across the back of Michelle's contemporary

designed terraced house. She was stood behind the

kitchen unit in a pale pink silky dressing gown,

dishing up eggs benedict for the two of them and

casting her own opinion upon Murray's day ahead.

"It sounds like the perfect job for your deceased friends! Isn't your Aunt just like you? I wonder why she hasn't gone along and solved the problem herself?" She placed the plates on the breakfast bar and sat down next to him.

"She could have done I suppose? She's better than me, she sees the dead never mind just hear them! I don't know why she's involved me... perhaps she didn't want to put herself between friends?"

"You don't think she suspects her friend?" Murray finished his mouthful, of the best eggs he'd tasted in ages, before he answered thoughtfully.

"No. She's pretty up front Aunt Pam, she'd have said if that was the case. Maybe she just thought I might need the work."

"Will Alistair and Rita help you?"

"Hopefully, if they turn up! I can't just call them in when I need them, but they would be useful. I'm not really sure what I'm going to do. Talk to the manager? Talk to the residents? The staff? Sort of warns the thief though."

"The manager won't do a discreet room search then?"

"Obviously not. According to Jo-anna the staff aren't taking it all that seriously, forgetful old dears and all that!"

"Bit patronizing."

With breakfast finished, Murray kissed his host goodbye and headed home. He wanted to finish his searches on the Wadebridge address and it's occupants before heading down to Tremeara. With the pangs of guilt returning during his drive home, the first thing he did when he got in was text Jenny's number. It was a quarter to nine so hopefully he would catch her before she started her first meeting. He just sent a simple message hoping her head was better and saying he would bring over her favourite dish from the Spice Palace when she got home... And of course, he sent his love.

Sat at his desk, he looked again at the names of the residents who lived at the large house in Wadebridge. Mr and Mrs Nigel and Kerry Stanford. Was Smith really Nigel Stanford? And if so, why hadn't Kerry Stanford reported her husband missing? Murray started with the marriage certificate, it should give their ages which would either match with Smith's or not. It turned out they had been married just six years, Nigel being noticeably older, by some eight years. Murray reckoned Smith was in his late thirties which did tie up with the thirty seven year old Stanford but what of the wife? He wondered if she was blonde... and short enough to position her car seat well forward? Were they a husband and wife team that committed theft to keep themselves in a nice house and lifestyle? Were they friends of the Whiteshaws who they helped commit an insurance fraud? Maybe the Whiteshaws were at risk of losing their Spanish villa? As Murray's mind raced through summersaults his phone rang.

"Murray Barber, private investigator."

It was Officer Barker. He was just about to start his

shift but as he had quickly re-read the reports on Mr Smith the evening before, he thought he'd call Murray while it was still fresh in his mind.

"Great. Erm... firstly, what do you make of Mr Smith? Do you think he's a long time felon?"

"Ha! No." Barker was laughing. "I don't think so."

"Well did the burglary seem above board to you?"

"You mean genuine?... Mmm. Yeah. Not very professional though. Chance act maybe?"

"Surely it must have been committed by someone who knew the Whiteshaws, or at least knew they were away?"

"Maybe? No prints were left. Nothing much to go on... except the car."

"What did you make of Smith in the car? He obviously wasn't the driver."

"No. He was out cold in the passenger seat. No goods found in the vehicle either, although we don't actually know how long they had the car."

"Is there any possibility that the robbery was set up so to gain from the insurance payout?"

"What payout? The Whiteshaws didn't have any contents insurance. The only payout they got was for the car. Their credit is good, they weren't in any obvious need of money. I don't think they had any reason to fake anything."

"Oh right. Well that knocks that theory out the window... Er, right, I need to think some more then. Can I call you back if need be?"

"Sure, no problem."

"Thanks."

Murray hung up his phone and sat back. If the

uneasy feeling wasn't about a fraud, what was this case all about? He shook his head and glanced at the clock, he should get going. Shutting down his laptop, he grabbed his keys and headed out of the door.

He called his Aunt Pam on the way down to see if she wanted to join him but she declined saying she had guests but he should call in on his way home and let her know how he got on. She'd call Jo-anna and let her know he was on his way.

When Murray arrived he was shown through to the lounge by Tina, one of the full-time staff. There he found Jo-anna sat playing cards at the large table with her friends. She warmly welcomed him and introduced everyone.

"Murray this is Tom and Cathy, Darcy, Byron and

Lizzie. Thankyou Tina, could we trouble you for a cup of tea for my guest?"

"I'll bring the trolley in then you can help yourselves."

Murray sat himself down beside Tom who started dealing another hand of cards.

"You know how to play Rummy don't you young man?" He was dealing Murray a hand.

"Er..yes, not played for a while though. So, who wants to tell me what's been going on?"

"It was Darcy first, wasn't it dear?" Jo-anna looked across the table at the tiny framed woman.

"Yes, my gold cross disappeared from my dresser. I always put it away there every night, always!"

"Then, a few days later, my pocket watch was gone." Tom was a frail looking man with shaking hands.

"And Barbara's cameo too. Taken right off her finger that was!" Cathy then called across the room towards the two ladies tucked up in wheelchairs infront of the tv. "Right off your finger, that's right isn't it Barb?" One of the ladies nodded and waved but didn't say anything. "Bless her. She was quite upset at the time but she's starting to go a bit loco..."

"Starting? Huh!" Tom spoke in a light-hearted tone. "Right young man, your turn."

Murray had been casting his glance around the room but now turned his mind back to the cards in his hand.

"If he's any good he'll lay the seven. Hasn't Cathy over there got a ten?"

"Yes, but she's got the five and six of hearts too. What seven has our new friend got?"

"Club. He should lay it." The voices were coming from various sides of the table the first, that of a woman, came from behind his left shoulder. Well, if Ali and Rita weren't around to assist him, maybe he could rein in the help of the locals? He laid his seven of clubs.

"I take it there's no chance of any outsider's getting in and stealing things?" Murray asked still aware of the 'other' voices who continued to give a running commentary on the game.

"We all get visitors." stated Cathy. "But no-one has come recently that hasn't been coming here for ages. That is the odd thing about it. There's no-one new around!"

"You tell him old girl! See if the young mind can work it out! Oh, looks like Byron here is collecting queens and nines."

Murray wished he could just ask their 'invisible' guests what exactly was going on, but of course he wasn't going to do that to himself, how would he explain it to this lot? On the one hand however, he was keeping track of the game and the hints he was unwittingly being given. To win would hopefully prove to the living that he had a clever mind to solve their problem and prove to be intriguing to the dead as to how he was following their suggestions!

"I take it none of the items have been found, has there been any kind of search?"

"No, and no." Jo-anna spoke as she watched the

hands being played. "If our relatives found out our stuff was being gone through they'd hit the roof..."

"Only because they'd be worried about someone going through their inheritance!"

"Oh Byron! They're not all like that. If Tom's daughter knew her grandad's watch had been stolen she'd be the first to rip the rooms apart!"

"Oh let's not tell my Samantha, please!"

"And we don't suspect the staff I take it?" Murray continued.

"No, we don't think so. Not unless one of them has got into debt maybe?" Darcy had lowered her voice to a whisper.

"They're so cold they might aswell be travelling with Captain Scott!" Murray had counted at least five different 'voices' around the table and was wondering now how he could wangle a private conversation with them?

"It wouldn't be so bad but these are personal things, things that have memories and mean something. If it was just cash we would still be upset but ... well... more resigned to losing it I suppose." It was the first time Lizzie had spoken up. "I'm sorry, I've forgotten what your name is young man?"

"Er.. Murray."

"That's unusual. No wonder I couldn't remember it."

"Don't worry about our Lizzie Murray, she can be a bit forgetful sometimes too." Jo-anna winked at him across the table.

"Ok." Murray smiled back at her. "So, we have no

new people, no searches of rooms, bags or wheelchairs! And no explanations! Mmm."

"Winnie, is it a jack he wants? Darcy here has just picked one up."

"Yes Grace. He's got three jacks, eight, nine and ten of diamonds." The voice from behind his shoulder was recounting the cards in Murray's hand.

"So, what about previous residents?" Murray asked as he watched Darcy lay his needed jack back on the table. "When did Winnie and Grace leave?"

"How does he know our names? Grace who is he? How does he know us?"

"Don't panic Winnie! He must be one of those psychics. He must be able to see us!" Unbeknown to Murray, he was now being stared at from all sides but he wasn't flinching when they started waving infront of his face. "No... no he can't seem to see us."

"Winnie and Grace? Blimey! They died...what two, maybe three years back now. What on earth made you think of them Murray?" Tom sounded astounded.

"Oh, names just popped in my head." Murray smiled. At least he now had their attention.

"He must know we're here. But how?"

"Don't be silly, we're dead, he's not!"

"You think he just guessed our names out of thin air?"

"No!"

"Sometimes Tom, your ears hear what your eyes can't see!" Tom stared at Murray bewildered but

Murray just smiled, the words were meant for different ears.

Unable to collect his needed jack, Murray picked up the seven of diamonds and laid his hand down on the table just as lunch was called. He declined their offer to join them and instead said he would go in search of Karen and see what she had to say. He silently hoped his new-found followers would accompany him.

Indeed, as he paused in the hallway outside Karen's office, Murray heard the now familiar whispers belonging to the past residents of Tremeara.

"What is he going to do?"

"Should we try and guide him to the culprit?"

"No! It'll be more fun watching him work."

"Maybe we could send him in circles? That'd be quite a lot of fun too!"

"Ok you lot!" Murray spoke in a hurried whisper. "I may not be able to see you but I can hear you." There were a couple of gasps followed by silence. "Call me whatever you want but I'm here to help these people get their things back. Their precious things. Will you please help me?"

"Why should we?" A woman spoke, it could have been the voice of Grace.

"It's not for me, it's for them."

"But we were hoping to watch you work."

"Please. Do you know who is stealing these things?" Murray pleaded, still in a whisper as he stared around the empty hallway.

"Maybe we do, maybe we don't?"

"Yes we do!"

"Sshh..."

"Oh come on!"

"You're our entertainment today. We're not letting you off that easily."

"So you do know who's responsible then?"

"We do. But what are you going to do about it?"

"Why don't you want to help? Don't you lot like these old dears?"

"Oh the cheek! We were once 'old dears' here as you so kindly put it!"

"So why won't you help them?"

"Maybe we are..."

"Mr Barber? You're a friend of Jo-anna's aren't you?" Karen had opened her office door and now stood welcoming him inside.

"Hello. Yes, well sort of. She's a friend of my Aunts. Thankyou for your time."

"No problem. I understand they've ganged up and engaged your services!"

"Something like that. Although I'm not sure how much I can help them."

"Mmm. Well let me assure you, I'm not ignoring their concerns. The last thing we want is for our residents to feel vulnerable... please take a seat." She gestured to the two seats infront of her modest desk. "Some things have been reported to me as missing. And I do take that seriously... but, well, the situation here hasn't changed at all. No new members of staff. And why should I suddenly suspect my team, a good team aswell, of suddenly being light-fingered?"

"To be honest, I don't think they suspect the staff."

"Oh good. I'm quite relieved to hear that." Karen sat back in her chair. Murray could hear shuffling to the side of him, they had an audience but it was remaining silent. "If I start making searches of their rooms I have to make all sorts of reports and the paperwork... well. Why should they start stealing from each other anyway? They're a good bunch here. All get along. It doesn't make a lot of sense."

"No. I agree. But unfortunately, that doesn't tell us where the things are going. They are all small items. I suppose they could be getting 'lost'. You know, falling down between furniture and that sort of thing?"

"Ha! Antarctic!" Grace and her friends had a strange way of being helpful.

"It's a possibility. Thing is, when something like that is suggested they all gang together in defiance. Such a suggestion is an insult! They seem to think that 'misplacing' these things is not an option."

"Ah, got it into their heads this is a conspiracy?"

"You're starting to see my position Mr Barber."

"Murray, please."

"Well, feel free to hang around Murray, and if you do happen to pick up on anything please let me know."

"Of course. Thanks again."

As Murray stood once more in the hallway, he at least felt that there was an official awareness of the situation, even if it was somewhat motionless.

"You lot still here?" he asked the empty space around him.

"Might be?" A cough and a shuffle followed.

"I seem to be on my own here. I can't search, there's no way that lady would consider the use of cameras and you're not prepared to help me. What am I supposed to do?"

"You could have some lunch. Jolly good food here."

Murray let out a sigh. He had no idea where the missing items were or who was responsible for their disappearance. He decided that he wasn't going to provide a floor show for his audience but instead say goodbye to Jo-anna and her friends for now and hopefully get Ali and Rita to come back and sort the situation out.

Once out of Tremeara, to the disappointment of

Grace and friends, Murray headed back to his Aunt Pam's house. As he knocked upon the door, he wondered who her guests might be? It was a silly question really, for once inside he was met by an all too familiar greeting.

"Murray my man, where have you been?" Ali's cheerful voice sprang from the kitchen table.

"I could have done with you half an hour ago! What are you hiding here for? Why didn't you follow me out to Tremeara?"

"Hello Murray!"

"Oh hi Rita. You two must have known where I was going."

"Sorry. We've been talking plants and cooking with your Aunt. How is the case going? Have you worked out where all their things are disappearing to?"

"No. Karen's very nice but she won't search the place and I doubt very much she'll allow any sort of camera in there."

"Oh dear." Pam sounded sympathetic.

"So you want us to have a nose round then mate?"

"Feel free! And good luck with the others that are there!"

"What others?" Pam asked handing him a mug of coffee.

"Half a dozen former residents who are infuriatingly unhelpful!"

"Oh dear." Pam repeated.

"Why won't they help? Surely they know who's taking the stuff?"

"They do Rita. But they want to see me work, just for their entertainment!"

"But you can't do much if you can't search or record anything. What do you want us to do then Murray?"

"If you don't mind you two, could you go over there and either get some sense out of that lot or make your own search of the rooms? See if you can find the missing items, a pocket watch, a ring and a gold cross?"

"Should be easy enough. No worries man."

"Good luck is all I can say!"

CHAPTER SEVEN

Murray stayed at his Aunt's long enough to fill in as many details as he could about Tremeara and its residents, on both sides of life. He then headed home to change ready to pick up a curry from the Spice Palace and go over to Jenny's.

Dressed in a fresh shirt and jeans, Murray first gave Jenny a quick call in case she hadn't made it home yet. She had but would much rather spend the evening at his place as her house-mate was having a loud argument with her boyfriend and it wasn't going to make a lot of space for their somewhat more romantic night. He offered to pick her up on the way to the Indian and on the way back she filled him in on her trip and her mother's enquiries as to whether she was planning on attending her dad's birthday get-together which included his 'floosy'. Unfortunately she wasn't going to be away on the date of his birthday but decided she would tell them both that she was and go into hiding for a couple of days, save any more arguments all round!

As they dished up and relaxed on the sofa, she finally got around to asking how his case was going with Mr Smith.

"... is he still Mr Smith?"

"Sort of. I have a name but I'm not sure if it belongs to him yet."

"What is it and how did you come by it?"

"Err..." Murray reached across to the desk and picked up his notes. "Nigel Stanford. I took Smith for a ride in the car. We went to the scrap yard and I got him to sit in the crashed car..."

"He was alright with that?"

"Mmm. He said it 'felt familiar'. Whatever that

means! Then I took him up to Okehampton to the Whiteshaw's house. The one he was supposed to have burgled? And guess what?"

"What?" Jenny sat with her fork poised before her mouth.

"He knew the way better than me!"

"Really? So... he knows the Whiteshaw's?"

"Maybe. He did know which house they live in. So, anyway I thought I'd carry on and took him passed the site of the accident."

"And?"

"And... admittedly it was foggy and even I wasn't sure where the accident happened, but he didn't react at all." Murray sat forward and topped up their glasses. "So... then I just carried on a long the road until we hit Bodmin and then he started to feel like he knew where he was!"

"He knows Bodmin? So do you think he comes from there?"

"Well, he directed me out to Wadebridge and we ended up right outside this particular house. A very nice, big house!"

"He said he thought he was well off. Good clothes you said."

"Mmm. Anyway we knocked, but there wasn't any answer, didn't look like anyone was home."

"So what then?"

"I thought that was enough for then. I took him home and told him to sleep on it. See if he can put the pieces back together."

"Has he?" Jenny was staring questioningly into Murray's eyes.

"Don't know yet. That was last night. I did look up the names of the people who lived in the house though... Mr and Mrs Nigel and Kerry Stanford. But if that is who he is, why hasn't his wife reported him missing? And where is she?"

"And was she the driver of the crashed car? Or.. was he having an affair and was the driver his mistress? Maybe he had left his wife? Maybe she couldn't care if he was missing?"

"You're not being all that helpful now!" he smiled at her as she gulped down the last of her wine.

"Sorry, getting carried away! Have you called the house?"

"By phone? No, not yet. Had to help out Aunt Pam! Her friends in the home are 'misplacing' their things."

"Ah, did you find them?"

"Not yet! I'll go back tomorrow and sort it. What are you up to tomorrow anyhow?"

Jenny pushed her empty plate across the table and curled up beside him.

"I've got to go into the office and finish the paperwork... not sure why we still call it 'paperwork'?"

"Can't you do that from here? Send it by e-mail?"

"We can for some of it but he likes the security stuff, you know, whatever company it is, their private information, completed on the off-line system. Pain in the backside!" Won't take all day though. Why? You got something planned?"

"Not really. Just a bit more time with you."

"Ah sweet! Do you have another bottle?"

"Yes! Give us your glass." He took the glasses to the kitchen but once there found he wasn't alone.

"Murray mate." A whisper came from beside the fridge.

"Ali?" Murray whispered back.

"Sorry man, but we've had some success. I did a bit of snooping while Rita did some sweet talking to Arthur and the others."

"Arthur? Oh, one of Grace's friends I take it?"

"Yeah! She's a sweet old thing really, once you crack her outer shell."

"Really?"

"Yeah. Anyhow, we know where the goods are but it's a bit awkward."

"How do you mean?"

"It's one of the residents, but the poor old girl

doesn't know she's doing it. Few blanks in her memory!"

"Losing her marbles you mean?"

"You ok Murray hun?" Jenny's voice called through from the lounge.

"Yeah, just coming..! Tell you what Ali. Can you meet me at Pam's tomorrow morning and we'll all go over there and have a quiet word with Karen. Is that ok?"

"Sure man! Have a good night!"

"I plan to!" Murray took the opened bottle back into the lounge where he found Jenny sat at his computer. "What are you doing?" He placed her glass down on the desk.

"Just seeing if there's anything on the wife. Kerry Stanford. I'm just pulling up the marriage certificate..."

"Do you know all my passwords?" he joked.

"Mmm. Why, shouldn't I?" she smiled up at him.

"Mind out. What's it say?" Jenny got up and sat

back down on his lap as they shared the desk chair.

"Oh! Fancy that?" They both stared at the screen.

"Well, that's certainly a connection isn't it?"

Murray glanced up at Jenny as a thought ran

through his mind. If Maria had been a witness to

the Stanford's marriage, what was their connection?

Were they in fact sister's? If so, then he knew where

Kerry probably was... Spain! "I think I have a

second visit to make tomorrow. And I think I'll take

Mr Smith with me. Maria didn't want to meet him

before and now we wonder just what her reason

was?"

"You think she doesn't want him to remember her? Surely if you're a witness to someone's wedding you know them pretty well? You'd think she wanted to help him?"

"Mmm. So we need to find out her reason for not. One thing is for sure, Maria Whiteshaw know's exactly what this is all about and exactly who our Mr Smith is."

"And why he robbed her?" Jenny picked up her wine.

"If he robbed her? I'm not all that sure there ever was a robbery."

"Really?" She switched off the computer and led him by the hand back to the settee. "Well, that's enough of them for tonight anyway. We've got better things to do..."

CHAPTER EIGHT

Jenny got up early the next morning and headed

into the shower. Murray managed to pull himself

out of bed and get to the kitchen to put on the kettle

and search for some kind of breakfast to offer Jenny

before she went to work. He found half a jar of

marmalade which he thought would be just perfect

to go with the home-made muffins that his Aunt

Pam had packed him off home with the previous

day. He stuck them in the oven to warm through

while he poured out the coffee.

"Thought you might have joined me?" she smiled as she finally entered the kitchen, dressed ready for work.

"Sorry. Thought I ought to take a turn with breakfast." He served up the muffins. When breakfast was over Murray dropped Jenny off at the station and headed to Pam's.

Ali and Rita were there waiting for him and along with Pam, they set off for Tremeara. During the car ride, Murray was filled in on the details of what had been going on. By the time they arrived, he knew who had taken the items and where they were but not, unfortunately how they were going to deal with it. It was decided in the end that Pam would have a quiet word with Jo-anna and get her to discreetly go and retrieve the said items, Murray would then go and have a chat with Karen and explain what was going on. He wasn't quite sure what he would say if she asked him how he had found it all out, but he was sure he would think of something...

While Pam went on in to have a quiet word with Jo-anna and Ali and Rita went in search of their new friends, Murray stayed in the car and rang Mr Smith.

"Hey, Smith?"

"Yes? Is that Murray?"

"Yeah, how you doing?"

"Not bad. I went back to Bodmin on the train yesterday, just for another wander round..."

"Really? Any good?"

"Well, the strangest thing happened, this guy came up to me outside the Town Hall and asked how I was! He knew me! Called me Nigel! Apparently my 'wife' has said I'm doing some work out in Spain!"

"Nigel? That ties in with what I found out yesterday too. I looked up the names of the people who live in that nice house we ended up. Nigel and Kerry Stanford. Do you feel like a Nigel?"

"I felt like a right Nigel when that guy was talking to me I can tell you! I had to try and explain to him that I've had no memory for the last five months. He took me for a pint and let me talk it out with him."

"What did he tell you about yourself?"

"What didn't he tell me? He thought at first I was winding him up! My name is Nigel Stanford, I'm thirty seven and I'm married to Kerry who's a bit tasty apparently! And I have my own business, some development company of some sort, I have a manager anyhow. See, I told you I had good clothes and I'd be able to pay you!"

"Good! But do you remember any of this now?"

"No. Pity. But no, I don't actually remember 'me' yet."

"Well, If I can pick you up this afternoon I would like to take you to see Maria Whiteshaw, the lady who's car it was?"

"Ok. Any particular reason?"

"Erm... I think she can explain what happened to you that day of the accident. I don't think you burgled her and I don't think you stole her car, but we'll see what she says later."

"What time have you arranged to meet her?"

"I haven't. I want to catch her unawares. I'm on

another job at the moment so if it's alright with you,

I'll pick you up when I'm done here?"

"Oh, ok. I'll be waiting for you then."

With the call over, Murray left his car and went in

through the front door of Tremeara where he was

instantly met by some welcoming voices.

"At last! Here he is!"

"Doesn't look like we're going to get to see our

floor show."

"No. No great detective at work. I'm quite

disappointed."

"Look you lot, there really wouldn't be anything to

see if I did do anything. I just sit and watch or put

in hidden cameras on a job like this."

"Well, we're not impressed."

"Well I'm sorry about that but at least you talked

to my friends last night, thank you for that."

"They asked nicely."

"I asked nicely! I pleaded."

"Not as nicely as Rita. She's a lovely young thing..."

"Arthur behave! She's much too young for you so don't make a fool of yourself!"

"Where are they anyhow?" Murray glanced along the corridor through the lounge door. But then he heard footsteps coming down the staircase and Joanna appeared from the stairwell. Murray smiled at her as she held out a hand full of the missing trinkets.

"They were just where Pam said they would be! How did you know?" She was staring with awe at him.

"That's a private eye secret! At least we can give

them back... mind you it might be better to give them to Karen to hand back quietly."

"Oh yes. We don't want to upset poor Lizzie. Bless her, she has no idea what she's been doing."

"I'll take them into Karen if you go and get Pam for me."

"Ok dear."

She wandered off in the direction of the lounge. Murray glanced once more around the empty hallway listening for the movements of Grace, Arthur and friends.

"Alright Murray mate?" Ali's voice sprang out from nowhere.

"Ali? Where did you come from?"

"We were upstairs with Jo-jo. How's Smith?"

"He's fine, I'll sort him out after we straighten this

mess out. I'll take Pam in with me. Hopefully Karen can deal with this in a gentle manner so no-one gets upset or offended."

"At least no-one's doing it maliciously."

"True Rita. Talking of malicious, where have our new friends gone?"

"I'm still here." It was a man's voice. "The others have gone to catch something on the morning programme."

"Arthur here is the one you need to thank, he told me about poor Lizzie and her night-time strolls."

"It's a bit like she sleep walks but not. But she really doesn't seem to remember what she's done."

"It might freak her out a bit if anyone tells her."

"Yeah, you're probably right Ali. We'll try and get Karen to go careful. Ah, here's Aunt Pam."

With the missing goods in their possession, the two

entered Karen's office and explained about Lizzie.

Karen in turn was more than grateful for them

coming to her rather than the group of residents.

She would deal with the situation in a discreet

manner and they shouldn't worry. Murray was just

grateful that they would get their treasures back. He

then drove Pam back to her home and headed off to

pick up Smith and sort out his situation.

CHAPTER NINE

It was a smiling Smith who jumped in alongside

Murray outside his lodgings. For the first time in

five months he felt like he was actually getting

somewhere, he was finally finding himself again.

The drive to Okehampton was upbeat but a little

apprehensive. Would Smith recognize Maria?

Would Maria co-operate? Murray had decided he

wasn't going to tell Smith everything he suspected

about Maria and Kerry and whether or not they

were sisters as he wasn't sure why they had decided

to shut Smith out of their lives? He had to admit to

himself that he didn't understand what was going

on in the personal relationships behind all the

drama.

They pulled up outside of the Whiteshaw's home

in the early afternoon with the sun shining for a

change. With a deep breath, the two men climbed

out of the car and strolled up to the front door. They could hear the sound of a washing machine spinning somewhere towards the back of the house as they rang the doorbell.

Maria answered the door. She stood stoney faced staring at Smith. It was the reaction that Murray had expected but he wasn't sure why.

"Mrs Whiteshaw I've brought Mr Smith here to meet you because I believe you know him quite well..."

Her glare turned towards Murray.

"I told you I didn't want him here. How dare you bring him here!" The anger was shaking in her voice.

"Do you know me?" Smith managed to keep his voice steady and firm.

"No I don't." snapped Maria.

"Oh, I think you do. You were a witness at his wedding to Kerry. Is she your sister? The one you've sent to Spain to keep out of the way?" Maria fell silent. She was studying Murray's face. "If Mr Smith here, or should I say Nigel? returns and waits in my car, will you let me in and talk to me?" After a moment's pause, Maria spoke.

"I don't want him in here." she said.

"Ok." Murray motioned for Smith to go and sit back in the car. Maria then let Murray inside.

They sat down in her cream-coloured lounge, Maria with her arms folded tightly across her chest.

"I wish you hadn't brought him here." she started.

"Is he your brother-in-law?"

"Unfortunately. He's one of those men that seem

so nice." her voice still shook. "He swept Kerry off

her feet but as soon as that ring was on her finger

she became his property. He managed to shut out

all her friends and had a good go at shutting us out

too. Completely controlled her, her whole life. She

couldn't step outside the front door without him

knowing her every move."

"So what happened five months ago? There wasn't

any robbery was there?"

"No..... no we made that up. It was a stupid thing

to do, we didn't really think out what we were

doing. We just reacted to what happened...."

Murray stayed quiet so to let her talk at her own

pace. "..She had stopped using her car. He was

clocking every mile she did in it and he would fly at

her if she didn't tell him exactly where she'd been. I

told her to take my car and park it away from the house so he didn't know she had it. I had told her so many times to just leave him and come and stay with us but.. well, I think she was just too scared... Anyway, then came the day of the accident. Which was all his fault by the way. We were in Spain and she had my car. But he must have been following her that morning because when she stopped the car up the road before coming home, he was waiting outside the gate and he jumped in the car trying to take the keys from her. She managed to restart the car but he was already inside and even though she kept driving he wouldn't get out. They argued but she wouldn't stop even though he was screaming at her and lashing out at her... you should have seen the state she was in when we returned from Spain.

She called us after the crash and said she thought he was dead. I told her to take all of her stuff out of the car and get a taxi back to mine and wait for us. We took the first flight back, only just made it and had to pay for first class, but we weren't sure what to do. I decided to report the car stolen to keep Kerry out of it. Then we had to work out how he got the keys so we faked a burglary. Kerry was terrified when we heard he wasn't dead. You have no idea how much we wished he had been. .. But then of course, we found out he had amnesia. I thought it was put on at first, to try and get to Kerry, but as time went on we started to believe it and set about explaining Nigel's disappearance. Told the manager at the office that he was doing some work over in Spain for us. Joint bank accounts anyhow and

Kerry eventually returned to the house. We got her to have the locks changed just in case he turned up unexpectedly remembering who he was.... and then you turned up. I admit we had no idea how long we could have carried on with the charade." She sat back and stared at Murray. "So what now?"

"I don't know. I was hired to find out who he was. I can tell him that now but he doesn't actually remember himself. I would certainly suggest that your sister files for divorce and sets in motion the split of property and so on. Get an injunction out on him if necessary? He seems harmless enough now but there's no reason he won't suddenly snap back into the person he was."

"Mmm. She's staying in Spain for now. I don't want him near her."

"Surely a solicitor will sort it all out quite quickly for you? I'm sorry to have brought him here... I wish you had been up front with me to start with, I could have dropped the case."

"I suppose it's not really your fault... It would only have been a matter of time anyway."

"I'll leave you the address of his lodgings and I'll take him back there now and explain this all to him. Maybe in his present state he'll see what sort of person he was and do something about it? I'll tell him to wait to hear from your sister's solicitor as regards what happens next. Is that ok?"

Maria nodded and stood to show him out, taking the scrap of notepaper that he tore from his notebook with Smith's address on.

Murray threw his keys down on the side and slumped down on his settee. What a day! He was ready for a long soak in the bath and a relaxing evening with a bottle or two of Merlot. As he stared across the room he noticed his answerphone was flashing. 'Huh! More work.' he thought. Still, he got up and pressed the play button. The first message was from Jenny.

"Hi babe! On my way home in about twenty minutes, I'll pick up something on the way and bring it over. Text me if you want anything special. Love you!"

He smiled, ok a relaxing evening with Merlot and company, even better! He played the second message...

"Hi Murray, sorry but couldn't get through on your

mobile. I've had a really bad day, ran into my ex and his tart! If you're not busy tonight I could really do with some company? I can bring a couple of bottles over? Please get back to me."

Murray pulled his mobile out of his pocket. It had switched itself off. Had he forgotten to put it on charge?

"Oh bugger!"